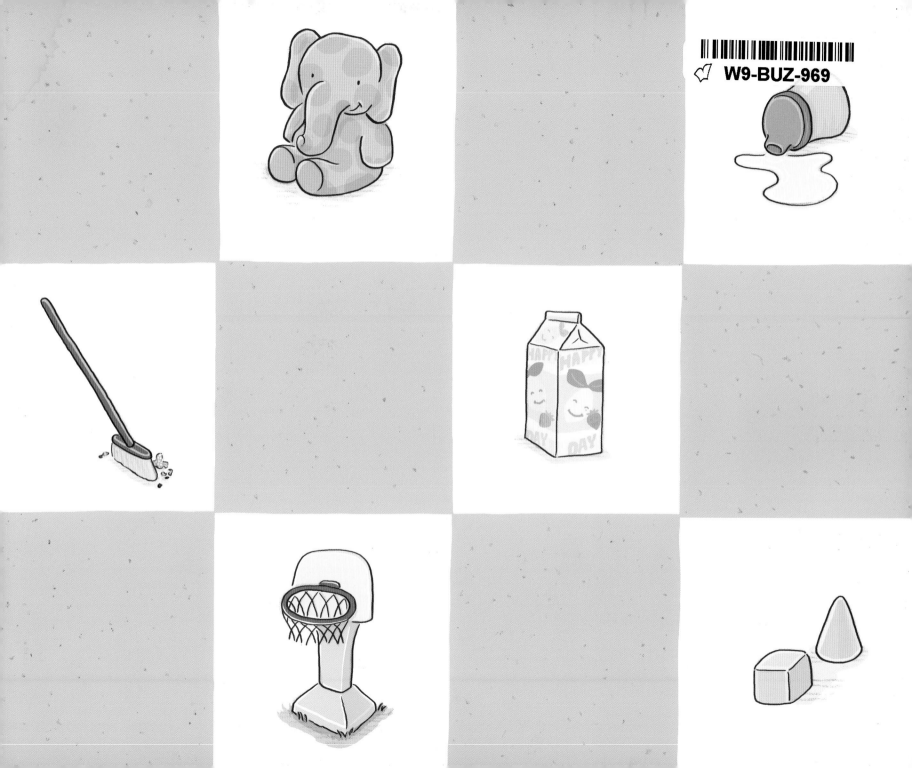

For all the really good dads

G. P. PUTNAM'S SONS

An imprint of Penguin Random House LLC, New York

G. P. Putnam's Sons is a registered trademark of Penguin Random House LLC.

Visit us online at penguinrandomhouse.com

Library of Congress Cataloging-in-Publication Data
Names: Gee, Kimberly, author, illustrator. Title: Mine, mine, mine, yours! / Kimberly Gee. Description: New York: G. P. Putnam's Sons, [2021] | Summary: Illustrations and easy-to-read text portray a busy toddler playdate full of playing, taking turns, sharing, and more. Identifiers: LCCN 2020044063 (print) | LCCN 2020044064 (ebook) | ISBN 9780593112403 (hardcover) | ISBN 9780593112427 (kindle edition) | ISBN 9780593112410 (ebook) | Subjects: CYAC: Play—Fiction. | Friendship—Fiction. Classification: LCC PZ7.G2577 Min 2021 (print) | LCC PZ7.G2577 (ebook) | DDC [E]—dc23 | LC record available at https://lccn.loc.gov/2020044063 | LC ebook record available at https://lccn.loc.gov/2020044064

Manufactured in China by RR Donnelley Asia Printing Solutions Ltd.
ISBN 9780593112403
10 9 8 7 6 5 4 3 2 1

Design by Marikka Tamura | Text set in Neutraface 2 Display | The art was drawn in pencil and painted digitally.

MINE
MINE
MINE
YOURS

Kimberly Gee

putnam

G. P. PUTNAM'S SONS

Come in,
come in,

come in . . .

go out!

Hide, hide, hide . . .

find.

Stop,
stop,
stop . . .

go!

Over,
over,
over . . .

under.

Jump,
jump,
jump . . .

bump!

Sorry, sorry, sorry . . .

that's okay.

Mine,
mine,
mine . . .

yours.

Yours,
yours,
yours.

Mine!

Messy, messy,

messy . . .

clean up.

Bye, bye, bye, bye, bye . . .

BYE!

Come

again!

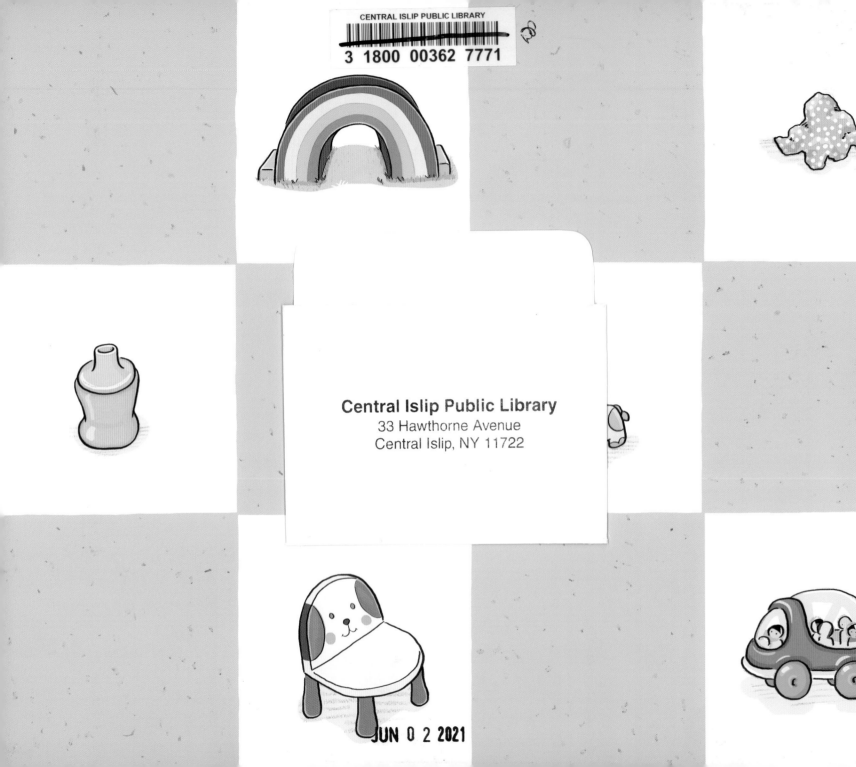